INVENTING TANIKAWA

谷 川 俊 太 郎 を 発 明 す る

詩

WILLIAM I. ELLIOTT

絵

CAROL ELLIOTT KALLISTA

訳

西原克政

MINATONOHITO

港の人

CONTENTS

FOREWORD

まえがき

06

CREEPY CRAWLER

もぞもぞ這うもの

16

RUN-AWAY BOOKS

脱走する本たち

18

SPEED TRAP

スピード違反

20

DOUBLE DECKER

ダブルデッカー

22

NO HITCHHIKING

ヒッチハイク禁止

24

BLACK DIAMOND

ブラック・ダイヤ

26

WC

トイレ

28

RADIO TINKERING

ラジオの修理

30

NO SPEEDING

スピード運転禁止

32

LUBE JOB

注油作業

34

TALL TIRES

タイヤが伸びる

36

DOUBLE BUBBLE

二重の泡

38

POET – COMPOSER

詩人と作曲家

40

TRICKS OR TREATERS

いたずらかおごりか

42

FIRST GREAT GRANDCHILD

最初のひ孫

44

BEACHY KEEN

ビーチのすがすがしさ

46

UNLESS SOUL SING

魂が歌わないと

48

CO-CONSPIRATORS

協働共謀者

50

INVENTING TANIKAWA

谷 川 俊 太 郎 を 発 明 す る

FOREWORD

The wheelchair is even older than Tanikawa Shuntaro – older by some 5,000 years. So, too, is the first chair itself which may have been a boulder or a tree stump. Chair and wheel, separately or adjoined, are, then, both older than this poet. For evidence we look to the arts of such distant times and climes as Mesopotamia and China, Spain and Germany. In relatively recent times we find that the third president of the United States, Thomas Jefferson (1743-1826) lays claim to attention. He invented a wheel-bed as well as castors for fitting to the bottoms of a chair's legs. Now well into the twenty-first century, wherever we look the kinds and uses of wheelchairs are almost innumerable.

For all its longevity and staying power, however, poetry is older than even the chair, the wheel and Tanikawa Shuntaro, either separately or in combination. Once more we must look back into the historic mists and myths of Egyptian, Mesopotamian, Babylonian, Chinese

まえがき

　車いすは、谷川俊太郎の年齢をこえるはるか昔からあったものである。その誕生はおよそ5千年の年齢差があるらしい。同様に考えると、この世に生まれた最初の椅子とは、おそらく巨石か木の切り株だったのだろう。椅子と二輪車は、別々でも接合されていても、両方ともこの詩人より当然年季が入っている。たとえば、はるか昔のメソポタミアや中国、スペインやドイツのような地域の工芸にその存在のありかを探し求めることができる。比較的近年だと、アメリカ合衆国第三代大統領トマス・ジェファーソン（1743-1826）がなんといってもその功労者にふさわしい。椅子の脚の底部にぴったり合うキャスター付椅子と同様、車輪付ベッドを発明したのは、彼だった。そして今や二十一世紀に入り、どこを見まわしても、車いすの種類も用途もほとんど数えきれないほどある。

　しかし、長い寿命と耐久力があるにもかかわらず、椅子、二輪車そして谷川俊太郎が、別々でも一緒でも、長い年月を越えて生き続けてきたにしろ、詩の歴史はそれよりはるかに長いものである。ふたたび、エジプト、バビロニア、中国やギリシアの歴史的靄のかかったはるかかなたの神話世界を振り返って、しごく当然なものを見つけださねばならない。

and Grecian histories to find something that should not be very surprising: poetry is older than the wheel, the chair and, of course Tanikawa Shuntaro. Is anything, any man-made tool or artefact, older than the use of language for what we might call humane purposes?

Words emerged in pre-history. Why words came, common sense tells us. Where they came from we do not know. This in in part a historically recent philosophic enquiry. It is surmisable that first words were utile in advancing human interaction and were expressive of thought and feeling. We can surmise that when utterances were still merely guttural that they narrowed into repeatably chanted formulas; namely, something like pristine prayer, mantras, hymns or other instruments of thought and feeling like hope and desire; in short, poetry, if not yet poems. Poems were, however, early in the making. Words were incipiently in the making of humankind proper. Whether we ask or do not ask, words came; they came and come as both questions and answers - how else? - in the form of words.

From another point of view we could say that words are a reverse 'ma,' long, noisy interruptions of silence which is at the heart of

つまり詩とは、二輪車、椅子、そして谷川俊太郎よりも長い時間を生き延びてきた。人間が作り出した道具あるいは手工品などのどんなものも、いわゆる人間の目的のための言語の使用よりももっと古いといえるだろうか。

　言葉は先史時代に誕生した。言葉がなぜ生まれたかは常識が教えてくれるが、どこからやってきたのかわれわれは知らない。これが多少とも近年の歴史的な哲学探究の成果である。言葉が最初に人間どうしの相互関係を推進するのに役立ち、思考と感情を表現できたことが、現時点からでも推測できる。しかし最初に口から発せられた言葉は喉頭音だけで、繰り返される短い単調な詠唱の文句、つまり原始の祈り、マントラ、賛詞、あるいは希望や願望の思考と感情を込めたその他に用いられる楽器の代用のようなもの、ようするにまだ一篇の詩にはなりえない通称の詩と呼ばれる類であったろうと思われる。一篇ごとの詩という作品が作られるには、まだまだ早い時期だったのである。けれども言葉は人間固有のものとして共に発達をとげてきた。その由来を問おうが問うまいが、言葉は生まれた。言葉は誕生し、問いと答え両方としてある。ほかのいい方としてはなんだろう。言葉の形式として言葉が存在している。

　見方を変えると、言葉は「間」に対立するもので、われわれの存在の中心にある沈黙をかき乱す長くて騒々しい横槍である。言葉の起源をた

our existence. It is in that deep and underpinning silence that words originate. Is it? Who knows?

The *Asahi* newspaper columns that Tanikawa Shuntaro has been supplying monthly for a decade and in fact the entire output of his poetry starting at the age of seventeen are a perplexed plumbing of that silence. The poems in the column entitled "Where do words come from...?" continue to ask an unanswerable question. Tanikawa finds that words are, after all, circular, turning back on themselves and headed nowhere but towards an impenetrable place of silence, and that is a place for which the Japanese language is as good a guide as humans are apt ever to find.

Surely Tanikawa would agree that he is word-challenged and not word-challenged, he who for now more than seventy-eight years has immersed himself and us in an ocean of words in which we still have, albeit, our heads above water. He is partially leg-challenged, as well. He negotiates some of the rooms of his house by a modest wheelchair such that in him we have a wheelchairful of words, past, present and future. His chair, his wheels, his words - his poems -

どると、その深い根底にあるのが沈黙なのである。はたしてそうだろうか。
ほんとうのところはだれにもわからない。

　谷川俊太郎が月一回 10 年以上にわたって掲載している朝日新聞への寄
稿や十七歳以来より始まった膨大な作品の創造の集積は、あの沈黙をふ
さぐための突貫工事の連続の賜物である。書き下ろしの詩を連載してい
る朝日新聞の「どこからか言葉が」の作品は、答えのない問いを発し続
ける。言葉というものが究極的に円環的で回帰するもので、ほかの場所
ではなく侵入不可能な沈黙の領域へと向かっていく、そしてそこがひと
にとって日本語という言語が良い案内人になれる場所であると、谷川自
身が気づいている。

　確かに谷川は、自分が言葉に憑かれているし、言葉に見放されてもい
て、いまや 78 年以上にわたって自分自身そして翻訳者であるわたしたち
を含めて、言葉の海に身を浸してきたことを自覚している。そのなかで、
われわれは水面の上に頭だけ出してなんとかかろうじて溺れないように
している。谷川はいま脚への試練も課せられている。家のなかの数部屋
をひかえめの車いすで行き来する彼の日常のなかから、われわれは過去・
現在・未来の車いすの言葉を紡いだ。彼の椅子、二輪車、言葉そして彼
の詩すべてが、先史時代と現代史を通って 2024 年までの時の流れを指し

all point back to pre-history and to modern history on up through 2024 when sitting in a rolling chair, instead of on a rock, there come bubbling out words interrupting that Ur-silence which is without end or beginning.

With the wheelchair as the metaphor of this book, he resurrects who we were, are and will be. Pre-history is preserved and nourishing. The book, then, is a tribute to Tanikawa Shuntaro, poetry (word), chair and wheel, and is meant to be, while containing visual and written elements both factual and fictional, a serious and amusing sally into his life.

Carol Elliott Kallista

Nishihara Katsumasa

William I. Elliott

示しながら、いまこの時、巨石のかわりに車いすにすわっていると、始まりも終わりもない原初の沈黙をかき乱す言葉がふつふつと湧き出てくるのである。

　車いすをこの本のメタファーにして、彼はわたしたちの過去と現在と未来の姿を浮かびあがらせてくれる。先史時代が保護され知的養分を与えてくれる。かくして本書は谷川俊太郎、詩（言葉）、椅子と二輪車に捧げる感謝の贈物であり、視覚と言語の表現には虚実が織り交ぜてあるが、彼の人生への真摯で滑稽な省察のつもりであることを付け添えておきたい。

キャロル・エリオット・カリスタ

西原克政

ウィリアム・I・エリオット

INVENTING TANIKAWA

谷川俊太郎を発明する

CREEPY CRAWLER

A chap name of Shun found his calling.
Another called Bill – O appalling!
Shun rode high in air,
Bill's cupboard was bare.
He ended up hungry and crawling.

もぞもぞ這うもの

俊という友が天職を見つけたとたん
ビルという彼の友がおやまあびっくりぎょうてん！
俊は天下に鳴りひびく
ビルの懐はさみしく
お腹もひもじく這うのがいちばん

RUN-AWAY BOOKS

All space has run out, so it looks.

All shelves in all rooms, even nooks.

He's lost all control,

tomes have taken their toll.

He's saddled with run-away books.

脱走する本たち

スペースはもうないそのよう

どの部屋も隅っこもすべて本棚のよう

こりゃこまったしまった

本たちはその本文を忘れた

脱走する本たちとの生活が始まったよう

SPEED TRAP

Not a notorious rover,

though he pub hopped from Shanghai to Dover.

And he challenged his mettle,

floor-boarded the pedal

and was ticketed twice for 'speed over.'

スピード違反

悪名高き海賊でなくて

上海からドーバーまでパブを渡り歩いて

勇気を奮い立たせ

ペダルを床まで踏み込ませ

「スピード違反」のチケットを二度も切られて

DOUBLE DECKER

An amanuensis named Korth

searched up and down, back and forth.

When she wanted a rest

she looked east and west.

She also looked south, but went north.

ダブルデッカー

［オフ・］コースという名の代筆者
右往左往にさがしもの
とにかくひと息つきたくて
西と東を見渡して
南を見て北へ行くぞと決めたものの

NO HITCHHIKING

To get to the reading, woe betide,

he struggled, he hurried, he hied;

when kind fate stepped in

as kind Shun leapt in,

pulled over and gave him a ride.

ヒッチハイク禁止

むべなるかな読み物に手を伸ばすには

あくせく苦闘しあわててあせるとは

やさしき運命が寄りそって

やさしき俊が乗ろうとして

車は止まって走りだすとは

BLACK DIAMOND

It isn't just what it may seem,
slaloming the slope, for this team.
But, yes, it's inviting,
amazing, exciting,
and even more so in his dream.

ブラック・ダイヤ

見た目とちがって
このチームのためこそ坂をエンヤコラって
それでも魅力的
驚異的　刺激的
夢の中ではそれにさらに輪をかけて

WC

A man's home is his castle, 'tis true.

He can even make up bathtub brew.

He decides what is legal:

hare, turtle and eagle

can join in his wc queue.

トイレ

にんげんのお家がお城とはなるほどね

自家製のビールもおちゃのこさいさいだしね

法律もひとが決めたもの

ウサギ、カメ、ワシの

トイレの順番待ちだってオッケーだしね

RADIO TINKERING

Like Sapphic lines from old Greece
or a puzzle that's missing a piece,
a wire went missing
and Philco went hissing
static that sounded like geese.

ラジオの修理

古代ギリシアのサッポーの詩のように
ワン・ピースなくなったジグソー・パズルのように
針金が一本なくなって
フィルコ製ラジオはうなり声の文句となって
雑音はまるでガチョウの声のように

NO SPEEDING

At racing he sure was no ace.

He usually came in last place.

The old hare was kind

to follow behind.

The turtle had finished the race.

スピード運転禁止

レースだとエースになるのはどうみてもむり

ビリになるのは予想どおり

むかしウサギはビリになっても

情けは深いとも

カメははなからレースを終えており

LUBE JOB

A squealing lawn mower in revolt
spits out rusty grindings and jolts.
So a wheelchair in pains
by squeaking complains,
"Oil up my screws, nuts and bolts!"

注油作業

芝刈機が反抗のきしる音を立てる
錆びた仕事と動揺を吐き棄てる
車いすも骨折り
きしんで鳴り
「ねじとナットとボルトには油を入れる！」

TALL TIRES

The idea vaguely appealing,

he wondered what would be the feeling

to rise to the sky.

He gave it a try

but barely arose to the ceiling.

タイヤが伸びる

想像はおぼろげながら魅力にみち
空まで上がってゆく感覚とはどんな気持ち
ためしにやってみた
がほとんど天井までも届かなかった
ちょっとだけ背伸びした心持ち

DOUBLE BUBBLE

Eye of newt and poison grub,

witches' brew of lethal slub,

Shun at home,

Macbeth the tome,

bubble bathing in a tub.

二重の泡

イモリの目と毒物

魔女の毒薬スープの飲物

俊は家に

「マクベス」は本に

浴槽の泡につかっているもの

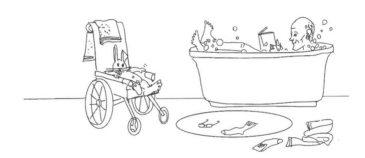

POET - COMPOSER

Shuntaro sings, Kensaku cuts

CDs. Such musical mutts!

All 'cross the land

one night stand after stand

they spent year after year on their butts.

詩人と作曲家

俊太郎が歌い賢作がＣＤを制作する今日

ふたりはまさに音楽狂！

全国津々浦々ツァーの真最中

一晩興行のめくるめく旅道中

ふたりはすわっての長年のコンサートのたびに帰京

TRICKS OR TREATERS

When neighboring kiddies appeared

as Halloween duly neared,

omg, the surprise

alive in their eyes -

he wasn't the ogre they feared.

いたずらかおごりか

ご近所の子どもたちが姿を見せて

ハロウィーンが着実に近づくにつれて

ああ　驚嘆の色が

彼らの眼に踊っているが

彼は彼らが怖がる鬼ではなくて

FIRST GREAT GRANDCHILD

Great grandchild soon learned how to talk.

At some other things she would balk.

But once on her feet

was fast-footed fleet,

with great granddad happy to walk.

最初のひ孫

ひまごはすぐにしゃべりかたを覚えた

ほかのことではおしゃべりをためらった

しかし立って歩けるようになると

曾祖父といっしょに歩ける喜びと

一体となって足早の二艘の舟のようだった

BEACHY KEEN

See him sit there bare legged and preen,

his cocktail blue, ice pink and green.

The white sky is spacious

and ten times more gracious

than any finite pc screen.

ビーチのすがすがしさ

靴下もはかずすましてすわっているのを見るがいい

カクテルは青、ピンク、緑がひんやりまぶしい

白い空ははてしなく広がり

どんなパソコン画面より

なん十倍もありがたい

UNLESS SOUL SING

An old man's but "a tattered coat
upon a stick" is what Yeats wrote;
unless his soul sing,
clap and louder sing,
like Shun, on a triumphant note.

俊のように勝利の調べを奏でて走れ
手を叩きより声を大きく歌わなければ
魂が歌を歌わなければ
といったイェイツはふっきれ
老人は「襤褸切れをまとった棒切れ」

魂が歌わないと

CO-CONSPIRATORS

Five items he never need dust;
recollects them bust after bust.
They inhabit his brain
well out of the rain,
never subject to pigeons or rust.

* W. Elliott, K. Kawaguchi, K. Nishihara, K. Tanikawa, K. Kawamura

協働共謀者

埃をかぶることのない五人の肖像がある
胸像をひとつひとつ思い出してみる
それらは彼の脳内に棲みついて
雨にぬれないようにして
鳩のフンも錆をも忌避する

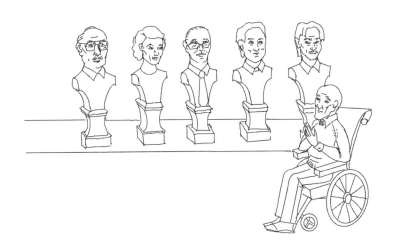

Carol Elliott Kallista lives in New York City. She spent forty years in the world of fashions both as executive and artist, and has published previous Tanikawa images in cooperation with her father.

Nishihara Katsumasa, now retired, is a specialist in American poetry and has translated poems of many Japanese and American poets, including some dozen books of Tanikawa Shuntaro. Also a critic, he has translated some of the work of the Japanese writer, Ibuse Masuji.

William I. Elliott, poet, shares Tanikawa Shuntaro's age. Both are 92. He is Carol Kallista's father. A poet, he and Nishihara Katsumasa have co-translated some twenty books of Japanese poetry, chiefly the work of Tanikawa Shuntaro.

キャロル・エリオット・カリスタ

ニューヨーク市在住。ファッション業界でエグゼクティブ兼デザイナーとして 40 年勤務する。父の前作『谷川俊太郎を想像する』(2015) でも、イラストを担当している。

西原克政

フリーランス翻訳家。日本とアメリカの詩の翻訳に従事してきた。とくに谷川俊太郎の詩集は 14 冊ほど手掛けている。近刊に井伏鱒二『対訳 厄除け詩集』(2023)。

ウィリアム I. エリオット

詩人、翻訳家。谷川俊太郎と同い年の 92 歳で、キャロル・カリスタの父である。西原克政とは日本の詩人の作品の英訳 20 数冊を出版している。谷川俊太郎の作品は約 70 冊をライフワークとして現在ほぼ全訳している。

INVENTING TANIKAWA

谷 川 俊 太 郎 を 発 明 す る

2024年10月5日初版第1刷発行

著者	William I. Elliott（ウィリアム I. エリオット）
絵	Carol Elliott Kallista（キャロル エリオット カリスタ）
訳者	西原克政
発行者	上野勇治
発行	港の人

神奈川県鎌倉市由比ガ浜3-11-49　〒248-0014
電話0467-60-1374　FAX0467-60-1375
www.minatonohito.jp

装丁	港の人装本室
印刷製本	シナノ印刷

©William I. Elliott 2024, Printed in Japan
ISBN978-4-89629-447-7